First published in paperback in Great Britain by HarperCollins Children's Books in 2006

1 3 5 7 9 10 8 6 4 2

ISBN-13: 978-0-00-718242-8
ISBN-10: 0-00-718242-2

Text and illustrations copyright © Emma Chichester Clark 2006

Visit our website at: www.harpercollinschildrensbooks.co.uk

Printed and bound in China

Melrose and Croc

FRIENDS FOR LIFE

by Emma Chichester Clark

HarperCollins *Children's Books*

It was spring, and
a day for singing.
"I am green!" sang
Little Green Croc.

"And I am hairy," sang Melrose.

"I wish I were as clever as you!" said Melrose.

"I wish I were as clever as you!" said Little Green Croc.

"You can do somersaults!" said Little Green Croc.

"And you can draw aeroplanes!" said Melrose.

"But I wish you were as tidy as me!"
said Little Green Croc.

"Well, I wish you were as quiet as me!"
said Melrose.

"And I wish you weren't so greedy!"
said Melrose.

"Well, I wish you weren't so greedy!"
said Little Green Croc.

"I like the way you listen to me when I'm talking,"
said Little Green Croc.

"I like the way you help me when I need you,"
said Melrose.

"I wish I could sing like you!"
said Little Green Croc.

"I wish I could dance like you!"
said Melrose.

"I like the way you put the toothpaste on my toothbrush," said Little Green Croc.

"I like the way you brush your teeth!"
said Melrose.

"I wish I were more like you,"
said Little Green Croc.

"But you are you, and I am me..."
said Melrose,

"…you wouldn't be you if you were like me!
There's no one else in the world like you!"

"No one like you and no one like me!"

sang Little Green Croc.

"I like us just the way we are...
friends for life!" sang Melrose.

Read about how Melrose and Croc first met...

Melrose and Croc

by Emma Chichester Clark

Hardback ISBN: 0-00-719729-2
Paperback ISBN: 0-00-722593-8

It is Christmas Eve, and both Melrose and Croc are all alone in the city.
They dream of a wonderful Christmas but feel sad for they have no one
to share it with. And so it might have been were it not for the sound of
beautiful music and a chance encounter. Could this be the beginning of
a happy Christmas and even the start of a wonderful friendship?

...and how they became the best of friends.

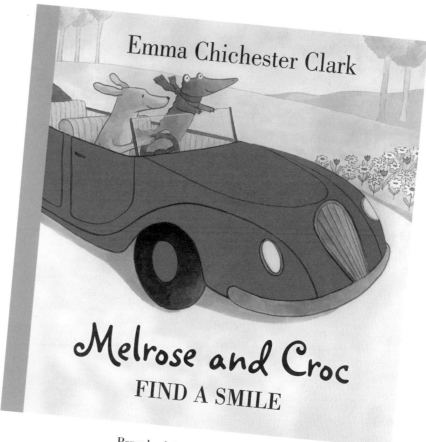

Emma Chichester Clark

Melrose and Croc
FIND A SMILE

Paperback ISBN: 0-00-718241-4

Melrose and Little Green Croc like helping each other. So when Melrose loses his smile, Croc decides to take him on a trip to the countryside. Maybe by hopping over a stream, catching a falling leaf and finding a special place to sit, they might just find it together.

Look out for other new titles about Melrose and Croc, coming soon!